GIFTS FROM THE SEA

BY NATALIE KINSEY-WARNOCK

ILLUSTRATED BY JUDY PEDERSEN

ALFRED A. KNOPF

NEW YORK

THIS IS A BORZOI BOOK PUBLISHED BY ALFRED A. KNOPF

Library of Congress Cataloging-in-Publication Data
Kinsey-Warnock, Natalie.
Gifts from the sea / by Natalie Kinsey-Warnock ; illustrated by Judy Pedersen.
— 1st American ed.
p.   cm.
SUMMARY: Quila and her father, living alone in a remote Maine lighthouse in
the 1850s, find their lives profoundly changed when a baby washes ashore
and they decide to keep her as part of their family.
ISBN 0-375-82257-7 (trade) — ISBN 0-375-92257-1 (lib. bdg.)
[1. Fathers and daughters—Fiction. 2. Babies—Fiction.
3. Lighthouses—Fiction. 4. Maine—History—19th century—Fiction.]
I. Pedersen, Judy, ill. II. Title.
PZ7.K6293Gi 2003
[Fic]—dc21
2002040725

Printed in the United States of America
June 2003
10 9 8 7 6 5 4
First Edition

*For treasured friends: Shirley, Chris, Shawn, Sara,
Nancy, Bill and Lucy, David, Lennie and Archie*

CHAPTER ✦ 1

A northeast wind was blowing the day we buried Mama on a hill overlooking the sea. I remember that particularly because I knew a storm was coming, had known it for days. Mama always said the sea was in my blood. Once, when I'd cut my finger, I'd tasted the blood and it was salty, so I guess she was right.

With Mama gone, that just left Papa and me, Aquila Jane MacKinnon, here at Devils Rock Lighthouse. I'd been born here twelve years before, April 18, 1846, and had never been anywhere else. If Mama hadn't taught me differently, I might have thought Devils Rock was the sum total of the world.

Devils Rock isn't an easy place to live. There's nothing here but birds and seals and the never-ending wind. Even though it's only five miles off the coast of Maine, fierce storms can cut us off from the mainland for weeks at a time. Sometimes we don't see another living soul for months on end, but at least when Mama was alive, she was always smiling and singing and it seemed we didn't need anyone else, we had each other.

We share the island with ghosts, too. Mr. Sinclair, the last lighthouse keeper, drowned rowing between here and the mainland, and Mr. Blair's wife went mad from the loneliness and flung herself off the cliffs. I've seen her shadowy figure moving over the rocks and heard her voice wailing above the wind. Before, I didn't understand how loneliness could drive someone crazy, but I was beginning to. Mama had only been gone a few hours and already I could feel the loneliness settling in for a long stay.

"The Lord giveth and the Lord taketh away," Papa whispered after Mama drew her last breath, but I was so mad at God I could spit. Seems he'd done a lot more taking away than he'd given. I was angry at Papa, too, though I couldn't tell him because he was already broken. I blamed him for Mama's death.

When Mama took sick, I'd begged him to take her to a doctor.

"Quila, you know I cannot leave the light unattended. Besides, your mother's strong. She'll be all right." When it became clear she wasn't going to get better, he would have rowed to the moon to get help, but it was too late.

The storm hit by evening and battered us for three days, howling and shrieking like a thousand banshees. I think Papa was glad for the storm, for he was so busy keeping the light burning that he had less time to think about Mama, but for me the storm was pure torment. I was trapped inside with all the memories of Mama pressing in so close I thought I'd suffocate: memories of Mama knitting by the fire, Mama coming in from a winter walk all rosy-cheeked and her blue eyes laughing, Mama singing me to sleep. Whenever I opened a book, the words came to me with Mama's voice attached, her stories of mermaids and pirates and kingdoms under the sea, and so reading brought no comfort. Neither did food. I baked bread, but when I pulled it from the oven, the warm, yeasty smell that had always been one of my favorites so reminded me of Mama that I threw it outside. At least the gulls would enjoy it.

Except for the wind, it was the quiet that near drove me mad. Always before, Mama had told stories, and if she wasn't telling stories, she was singing, and if she wasn't singing, Papa got out his fiddle and played "Blackbird," "Devil in the Kitchen," and "The Wind That Shakes the Barley" while Mama and I danced till we were breathless. Papa could make his fiddle moan like the wind as it snarled and prowled round the lighthouse tower, and I could never tell if he was answering the wind or if it was answering him. Even the seals came up on the rocks to listen, their dark bodies silvery in the moonlight.

Papa had never been one to say much—Mama said he let his fiddle speak for him—but when she died, Papa put his fiddle away and it was as if he'd lost his voice. Throughout the days of that storm, I never heard him utter a word. Me, I wanted to howl along with the storm.

When the storm finally blew itself out, I fled the silence of the lighthouse and ran to the cliffs.

Seabirds screamed and circled below me, thousands of them, jostling for nesting sites on the ledges. Soon there'd be thousands of eggs, and Papa and I would have eggs for breakfast, dinner, and supper. Mama and I'd always loved spring, when the sun was bright again, the birds came back to nest, and the wild geese flew north. Their haunting cries tugged at me and made me want to fly with them.

If Mama were here, she and I would have been combing the beach area for shells or brightly colored sea glass ("gifts from the sea," Mama called them) or searching along the cliff edges for all the tiny wildflowers, but I didn't have the heart to hunt for them myself. It just seemed another reminder that she was gone forever.

Out of habit, I scanned the horizon. I was good at spotting things, had "eagle eyes," Mama had said. That's what my name means, *eagle*. Papa had taught me how to read the water, how to tell where there were rocks just under the surface, for there were many such rocks surrounding Devils Rock, all of them dangerous, all of them waiting to bring ships to their doom. Papa had also taught me how to look for whale spouts, far

out to sea, or rafts of seabirds, which indicated a school of fish. By the time I was two, I was announcing ships before Papa and Mama could see them. But on this day, I didn't see anything out of the ordinary. It was as if the storm had scrubbed the sea clean.

It wasn't until I dropped my eyes that I saw something, something dark in the white froth of the waves. At first, I thought it was a seal, but when I saw a door float by, I knew a ship must have gone down in the storm.

Items were forever washing up against our island, items Papa managed to fish from the sea: chairs, coils of rope, barrels of salt cod and oil, shoes, and once a woman's parasol. I'd twirled that parasol on my shoulder, imagining myself strolling down a street in New York, or London, or Paris, until I'd felt an icy hand touch my shoulder and knew another ghost had come to live with us on Devils Rock. Mama may have wondered why I never asked to play with the parasol again. But we used the chairs, and cod, and coal that Papa pulled from the sea. It would have been wasteful not to.

I knew there were places, coastal communities, where people made their living from shipwrecks. They were called "wreckers" and used lanterns at night to lure ships onto dangerous rocks so the ships would sink and scatter their cargoes where the wreckers could "harvest" them. But I couldn't imagine such a life, luring people to their deaths just for their belongings. Finding items from shipwrecks only made me sad, and I always thought of those poor people and what their last moments were like. What did it feel like to drown, to scream and know no one could save you, to disappear beneath the waves, unable to breathe? . . . I shuddered and hoped I'd never find out.

I picked my way down the steep stone steps that some lighthouse keeper had chipped out of the cliff face. The object was a few feet offshore. I picked up a piece of driftwood and tried to fish it out, but it bobbed just out of reach. From what I could tell, it looked like some bedding with rope wrapped around it.

I lifted my skirts and waded into the water. I knew I was taking a chance; currents swirled around Devils Rock, that's one of the reasons it was such a dangerous place for ships, and it was certainly no place to swim. Papa would have my head if he knew I had as much as one toe in that water, but my curiosity was stronger than the swirling tide.

The current pushed hard against my legs. It was stronger than I'd expected; if I went down, I probably wouldn't be able to get to my feet again. I'd be swept under and Papa wouldn't know what had happened to me. I knew I should go back, but now I was close enough to see that the object was two tiny mattresses lashed together with rope. Why would someone tie two mattresses together? I took two more steps and was able to hook one end of my driftwood under the rope.

Once I was back on solid footing, my knees shook so, I almost fell. I stared at the odd bundle. I tugged at the rope, but I couldn't loosen it, so I picked up a sharp-edged rock and sawed away at the rope until it let go. My heart thudded fast as I pulled away the top mattress . . . and then I was pounding up the steps, screaming at the top of my lungs, "Papa! Papa! Papa!"

Papa met me at the cliff top, wild-eyed and shaken by my screaming. He grabbed my shoulders.

"Quila, what is it? What's wrong?" And before I could answer, a high, thin wail rose from below.

"A baby, Papa!" I whispered. "I found a baby."

CHAPTER ❧ 2

We named her Cecelia, which means *a gift from the sea*, but we called her Celia, and before long, we couldn't remember what life had been like without her.

Papa rowed to the mainland and brought back a goat so we'd have milk for her. I cut up an old sheet to use for diapers and had to keep water hot on the stove for washing them out. How I wished Mama were here to show me what to do and how to take care of her, but I did the best I could. I fed her, bathed her, rocked and sang her through bouts of colic, and told her stories of mermaids and selkies, those seal-like creatures that spirit children off to the sea, though it seemed this time that the selkies must have brought Celia to us.

For months after Mama's death, it was Celia alone who could bring a smile to Papa's face. He carved her a cradle from one of the ship timbers that washed ashore, but I'd often find him cradling her in his arms instead, crooning lullabies to her, and she'd gurgle something back at him that only he seemed to understand.

On nights when Celia refused to sleep, I carried her outside to show her the stars.

"There's Cygnus, the swan, and Pegasus, the flying horse, and that one over there, that's Aquila, the eagle." I remembered Papa holding me up to the stars, pointing out the one that had the same name as I did. I'd thought he'd put it up there just for me.

Papa appeared in the doorway.

"You should be asleep," he said. I wasn't sure whether he meant Celia or me.

"I was showing Celia the stars. Remember how you used to bring me out here?"

Papa acted as if he hadn't heard me. He lifted Celia from my arms.

"It's late," he said. "You go on to bed."

"She needs changing."

"I'll do it," he said. When I didn't move, he added, "I know how to change a diaper, Quila." Papa had never been snappish before Mama died.

"I know," I said. "It's just that . . ." I didn't continue. How could I make him understand that the Papa I'd known all my life had disappeared and I missed him, almost as much as I missed Mama? I'd always loved being his helper—"Papa's shadow," Mama had called me—and he'd seemed to love my company as much as I loved his, but all that was in the past now.

Papa slept so little that he often fed Celia at night so I could sleep, but mostly I took care of her so Papa could take care of the light.

There is a lot of work to "keeping a light." The lens has to be cleaned and polished, the brass casing of the lens and all the brass fittings polished, too, the reflectors cleaned of soot, the oil lamps cleaned and filled, the wicks trimmed, the floor and the stairs dusted with a hand brush, the windows of the lantern room washed, and all of that done every day. Papa climbed the stairs to the tower at least three times a day: at sundown to light the lamps, at midnight to check the oil supply and trim the wicks, and again at sunrise to blow the lamps out. In bad weather, he might go days without sleep. Every evening, the log had to be written up, recording weather conditions and any equipment problems or repairs, and every year, Mama and I helped Papa paint the lighthouse, a clean, shining white that took my breath away. Papa always said you had to tend the light like a baby because people's lives depended on it, and now I found out how much work tending a baby could be. Whereas Papa's life revolved around the lighthouse, mine revolved around Celia.

The days blurred together as if they were one, and I couldn't remember what it was like not to be tired. There was no rest even when Celia was sleeping, for then I had to be milking the goat or washing out her dirty diapers to hang by the stove so they'd be dry for when I needed them again. No sooner had I washed the dishes, swept the floors, and fallen into bed than Celia would cry and it would all begin again, heating the milk, feeding her, changing diapers, and rocking her back to sleep. And I could never go to bed without

making sure that the lens cover was clean and ironed for the next day.

Because linen does not scratch the lens the way wool might, all lightkeepers were required to wear linen smocks, and every morning (unless there had been a storm and the light was still needed) the lens was protected with a linen cover. Both the smock and the lens cover had to be washed and ironed without a wrinkle. Mama had never let me iron the linen, for fear I might scorch it. There was no choice but for me to do it now, but my mouth went dry and my hands shook every time I held the iron over the cloth.

Gone was my life of hiking along the cliffs, looking for ships and watching sunsets. I wondered if I'd ever have time for them again.

Mama had made keeping house look so easy. Caring for Celia was a full-time job, and there was the laundry, and sweeping, and mopping, and mending, and cooking on top of that. I ended up fixing meals that were easy and quick. If Papa grew tired of eggs, oatmeal, and fried fish, he never complained, but I was sick of them. Every bite was a reminder of how much I missed Mama's cooking: the fish soup called "cullen skink," crisp oatcakes baked on top of the stove, mealie pudding, and melt-in-your-mouth shortbread. My oatcakes looked and tasted more like shingles, and you could have cut glass with my shortbread.

We'd had Celia only a few months when Papa poked his head in the door to tell me to set an extra place at the table. Mr. Callahan's boat was in view.

Mr. Callahan was the lighthouse inspector. I'd always looked forward to the stories he brought us, like that of Abby Burgess, the daughter of the lighthouse keeper on Matinicus Island. With her father on the mainland getting supplies and medicine for his sick wife, a storm had washed away the keeper's house on the island. Abby had moved her mother and sisters into the light tower and kept the light burning for four weeks until the storm had passed and her father could return. Mr. Callahan had also told us of Mary Patten, who'd sailed her ill husband's ship around Cape Horn, and of the storm that destroyed the Minot's Ledge Light. The two keepers had been killed when the tower toppled into the sea, but they'd kept the light burning to the last.

We'd get so caught up in his stories that when the

clock chimed midnight, we'd stare at it in astonishment, certain that Mr. Callahan had only been talking a few minutes.

"Gracious, look at the time!" Mama would exclaim, and march me off to bed, where I'd lie awake thinking my heart's desire would be to travel from lighthouse to lighthouse, gathering stories at every stop.

Most lightkeepers were nervous about having the inspector visit, but we were always glad to see him. Mr. Callahan said Papa kept the best light along the whole coast of Maine and that he only stopped by Devils Rock to taste some of Mama's cooking. He especially loved her dried-apple pies.

I looked around the kitchen and felt ashamed. Diapers, washed but not yet dry, hung from doorknobs and over the backs of chairs. The floor was unswept, the breakfast dishes still dirty in the sink. Mama had always kept such a clean and tidy home and now Mr. Callahan would see what a poor housekeeper I was.

I only had time to set a bowl of dried apples to soak before I heard Papa and Mr. Callahan at the door. Mr. Callahan shook the sea spray off his oilskins and stepped inside, his face lighting up when he saw me. He handed me a package.

"This was at the post office, and I knew your mama would be eager to get it. I'm guessing it's more books."

Each year, Mama had ordered two or three new books that the lighthouse tender delivered when it brought our yearly supplies of coal and lamp oil, and those books were more precious to us than silver. We savored them, to make them last, but they never lasted long enough. But Mama's most treasured book was one Papa had ordered to surprise her, a copy of Mr. John James Audubon's *Birds of America*, all the way from London, England! It had been dreadfully expensive, a whole month's salary, but Papa said it was worth every penny to see the look on Mama's face. She and I'd spent hours poring over its pages, looking at the beautiful paintings.

I clutched the package to my chest. Mama and I wouldn't get to share these books.

"Mama died," I said. The words grated like gravel in my mouth. It was the first I'd said it out loud to anyone.

Mr. Callahan looked stricken. Celia began to cry, and her howls startled him.

"I didn't know you had a little one," he said. "I can see you've got your hands full. Looks like I ought to head down the coast today and stop at the Matinicus Light for supper."

I could picture Abby Burgess serving Mr. Callahan a delicious meal and telling him about her latest heroic deed. She'd probably saved a whole shipload of people by now, or rebuilt the living quarters at her lighthouse, all by herself. Besides, Mama would have been mortified at turning a guest away.

"Oh, no, Mr. Callahan," I said. "Please stay. I'll have supper ready soon, and I'm even going to make pie, though it won't be up to my mother's standards. I'm afraid I'm not the cook or the housekeeper she was."

Mr. Callahan looked down at Celia.

"Well, you're doing a fine job with that baby," he said. "She seems healthy enough."

I didn't tell him how thoughts came swirling into my head now and then, like waves around Devils Rock, of how much simpler my life would be if I *hadn't* seen that bundle of mattresses floating in the water. For certain, Abby Burgess would never have such horrible thoughts.

Mr. Callahan and Papa climbed the tower to check the light while I finished making supper. My gravy was lumpy, the carrots overcooked, and the piecrust soggy, but Mr. Callahan was a good sport and cleaned his plate.

Instead of stories, he and Papa talked politics, then went on to discuss lighthouse engineering, the merits of various lamp oils, and lens construction. I found such talk exceedingly dull and longed to get my nose in one of the books Mr. Callahan had brought. In my rush to get supper on the table, I'd only had time to peek at the titles: *Moby-Dick* and *Uncle Tom's Cabin.* Mama and I'd never had enough books. She'd told me she'd take me to a library some-day. A library was what I imagined heaven to be, rooms and rooms of books, enough to read through eternity. I wondered if Abby Burgess longed for books as much as I did. When I finished with the books Mr. Callahan had brought, maybe I'd send them on to Abby, and she could pass them on later to someone else. We could start a traveling library for lighthouse families.

Mr. Callahan's voice broke through my thoughts.

"What were you saying about a lighthouse library?" he asked. He and Papa were staring at me.

I hadn't known I was talking aloud and felt my face grow hot.

"I . . . I was just thinking there ought to be books available to the lighthouse families. Why couldn't a box be delivered to each lighthouse, and then when you visited, we'd trade our box with another light-house?"

Before the words were even out of my mouth, I wanted to snatch them back. My idea sounded foolish and childish. Why couldn't a wave appear right now and carry *me* out to sea?

Mr. Callahan cleared his throat and looked at Papa.

"Your girl's got brains," he said.

Pain slid across Papa's face.

"She got those from her mother," he said.

CHAPTER 3

Always before, Mr. Callahan had spent the night at Devils Rock, but this night he decided to go on to Matinicus Light. Had he stayed, Celia's near-disaster would never have happened.

Papa lit the lamps and settled in his chair to patch his boots. I washed the dishes quickly, figuring I'd put Celia to bed and begin one of the new books Mr. Callahan had brought, but Celia had other plans. She wasn't the least bit sleepy. The only way I could get her to sit still was to tell her favorite story.

There once was a fisherman who found he could make more money selling sealskins than fish, so he crept amongst the rocks and killed the seals while they were sleeping. He had great piles of sealskins in his house, and people came from far and wide to buy them.

One evening, a stranger rode in on a dark horse with a grey mane and tail. The stranger called out to the fisherman, "My master wishes to do business with you and asks that you come with me," so the fisherman climbed up behind the stranger and they galloped across the moors until they came to a cliff overlooking the sea. The horse never slowed, but leaped off the cliff, and they fell down, down, into the sea. At first all was darkness, but as they fell, the fisherman noticed a green light that got brighter and brighter until he found himself in a kingdom of sea-mountains and sea-forests. Seals were swimming all about, and when the fisherman looked down, he saw that he had been turned into a seal himself. The fisherman could hear the seals' voices but they spoke in a language he did not know.

The stranger, who was now a seal himself, led him into a sea-foam palace, and on a bed lay an old grey seal, moaning with pain. Next to him lay a bloody knife, and the fisherman was filled with fear when he saw it. It was his knife, and just that morning he had used it to stab a seal, but the seal had plunged into the sea, carrying the knife in its back.

The fisherman fell on his knees, begging for mercy.

"This seal is my father," the stranger said. "Only you can save him. Put your hand on the wound."

The fisherman did as the stranger ordered, and the wound healed at once.

"You may return to your home," the stranger said, "but you must promise never again to hunt seals. Go back to fishing, and our seal-folk will make sure that you catch many fish."

The stranger led the fisherman back to dry land, where he turned into a man again.

"Remember your promise," the stranger said, and disappeared beneath the waves.

The fisherman kept his promise. He went back to fishing and his nets were full every time he pulled them in, so his wife and children never wanted for anything, and he told his children and grandchildren about the kingdom of seals so that none of them would ever harm a seal.

Celia was asleep in my lap. I laid her in her cradle and was reaching for *Moby-Dick* when we heard a loud *Bang!* and the sound of glass breaking. Papa leaped up, upsetting his chair. He yanked on his boots and bounded up the winding staircase to the tower, me close behind him.

A lighthouse keeper has to be ready to handle any emergency, whether it be storms or shipwrecks, or broken equipment, but I daresay even Papa was surprised at what he saw.

He opened the door to the lantern room and stopped so suddenly I bumped into him. I craned my neck, trying to look around him, but he stepped forward, his boots crunching on broken glass. A large bird staggered across the floor, dragging a wing through the glass. Had I not studied Mama's Audubon book so thoroughly, I wouldn't have known it was a razorbill, for they were not a common sight along our coast.

Bang! I jumped and covered my head as more glass came cascading down around me, and another razorbill dropped at my feet. *Bang! Bang! Bang!* Bodies fell around me, piling up on the floor. I heard the whir of wings as more birds flew into the lantern room. Then they were caught, frantically beating against the windows from the inside. Their beaks clattered like stones against the glass. Papa climbed a ladder and, with a broom, was able to shoo them out through the broken panes.

Most of the birds at my feet had died on impact. Three were so badly injured that Papa knew they could not recover, and he quickly wrung their necks so they wouldn't suffer anymore. The remaining bird stood by itself, blood dripping from its breast. It stared at me, dark brown eyes unblinking. Papa reached for it and I couldn't bear to think of its neck twisting in his hands.

"Please don't kill it, Papa," I begged.

"I wasn't going to," Papa said. "I don't think it's badly hurt—no broken wings or legs, just a cut, and I think I can fix that."

Papa threaded a needle. I wrapped a towel around the bird and held it while Papa stitched up the ragged cut. It must have hurt terribly, but the bird never struggled or tried to bite, just stared at us. I hoped it knew we were trying to help it.

"Why'd they fly into the tower?" I asked. Papa shrugged.

"They may have been attracted to the light, or they may have gotten disoriented somehow. Luckily, they didn't knock out the light, but I'll have to see what the damage is."

While he climbed the ladder to check out the lens, I made up a box with a blanket in it and set the razorbill in its new bed. I got some fish from the kitchen, but the bird refused to eat, so I left the fish in the box.

The birds had shattered several of the prisms in the huge reflector. At daybreak, Papa replaced the glass panes in the lantern room windows, but new prisms were a different matter.

"I'll have to go to the mainland for those," Papa said, and I wondered why he sounded so worried until I realized he'd have to leave me alone. Only once had he left me alone, when he'd brought back the goat so Celia would have milk. Before that, whenever he'd gone for supplies, Mama had been here to tend to me and the light.

"You're too young," Papa said. "What if a storm comes up while I'm away?"

"Doesn't feel like a storm's brewing," I said. "Besides, Abby Burgess took care of her lighthouse for *four weeks*."

"Abby was seventeen at the time, and a very responsible girl."

His words stung.

"You don't think I'm responsible?"

Papa winced. "I didn't mean that," he said. "Of course you're responsible. I couldn't care for Celia without you. I only meant that you're still very young to be taking care of a light."

"I'll be fine, Papa," I said. My words did not reassure him, I could tell, but he was even more worried about the condition of the light. Devils Rock Lighthouse was his responsibility and it needed to be repaired before the next spate of bad weather hit.

"If I hurry, I ought to be able to get over there and back with no trouble," he said. He walked down to the boat and with misgivings in his heart and mind, he rowed away.

I wasn't really alone—I had Celia, and the razor-bill, to keep me company—but I felt giddy with the sense of freedom. I almost wished a storm *would* blow up and strand Papa on the mainland. I'd keep the light burning no matter how long Papa was away, and Mr. Callahan would tell my story up and down the coast and parents would use me as an example to their children.

"Now, that Aquila MacKinnon, she was a brave girl," they'd say. "She tended a light *and* a baby at the same time! Even Abby Burgess didn't have a baby to contend with!"

Celia's howls jarred me from my daydreams, but once I'd fed and changed her, she was her happy self again. She'd begun crawling and I had to watch her every second. Caring for Celia made me appreciate all the work Mama had had in raising me, for she'd said I was an adventurous, willful child with a mind of my own.

It was a rare day on Devils Rock, sunny and mild with just a hint of a wind. I left the door open to bring in fresh air while I worked. I surveyed the kitchen, looking at what needed to be done, the same chores that needed to be done every morning, and a voice inside said, "No, not today." And I knew I wasn't going to waste my day of freedom washing dirty dishes and diapers.

I looked out to where the sea joined the sky, and saw a boat in the distance. I watched it come closer, studying the movement of the oars, how the boat plowed through the water, and knew it was Mr. Richardson, a fisherman from the mainland. The way a fisherman handles his boat is as distinctive as his voice, and I always knew who was fishing off our light long before I could make out their faces.

"Hi there, lass," Mr. Richardson called out as he came close enough to be heard. "'Tis a bonny day, is it not?"

Tears stung my eyes, for *bonny* was a Scottish word Mama had often used to describe a beautiful day on Devils Rock. I could only nod.

I liked Mr. Richardson; he seemed more like a

grandfather to me, especially as I'd never known my real grandfathers. But he had a large red nose, doubtless made larger and redder by years of being frostbitten while at sea, and as he looked up at me, I remembered Mama's word for such a nose as Mr. Richardson had—"reefart-nosed," which meant having a nose like a radish—and a giggle started somewhere down in my middle. I tried to suppress it, for I couldn't be so rude as to be laughing at dear Mr. Richardson, but it fought its way upward and exploded out of my mouth. Poor Mr. Richardson began laughing, too, not knowing I was laughing at his expense.

"Oh, it's good to see you laughing," Mr. Richardson said. "We were grieved to hear of your dear mother's passing." At mention of Mama, his nose didn't seem funny anymore.

"My wife has been wanting me to bring you over for a visit," Mr. Richardson said. "It's such a bonny day, and I haven't had much luck with the fishing. Might you ask your father if he'd allow you to go today? I'll bring you back before nightfall."

My heart and legs leaped at his offer. I'm

ashamed to admit my first thoughts weren't about the light, how I was in charge and couldn't leave the light unattended. What I was thinking about was going to the mainland for the first time in my life, seeing streets and shops, riding in a carriage pulled by a high-stepping horse, seeing trees and gardens, and walking in a place where you didn't have to worry every step about falling off a cliff. It would be a day I would never forget. Then I remembered Celia.

"I can't," I said, the words like broken glass in my mouth. "I wish I could, but I can't." I didn't dare tell him Papa was away, for Mr. Richardson, dear soul that he was, would have felt obligated to stay until Papa returned. How would that convince Papa that I was capable of staying alone?

Mr. Richardson didn't ask for a reason, just nodded sadly and pulled away. I wanted to leap into the water after him, climb into his boat and sail away and never have to think of Celia again. I'd given up everything I loved, these last few months, to take care of her, and she was too young to even appreciate it.

Celia was the last thing I wanted to see right then, so I decided to check on the razorbill instead. I found the fish lying untouched in the bottom of the box.

"You have to eat," I said. I held the fish up to his beak, but the bird only stared at me, unmoving, unblinking. He might not be strong enough to fish on his own, but if he didn't eat what I offered, he'd die of starvation anyway. I decided to return him to the sea.

I carried the razorbill down the steep steps and set him on the water. He floated there, riding the waves, then curved his neck and dove under the surface in one smooth, liquid motion. I stared after him, wondering what it would be like to be a wild creature, to be able to swim or fly away wherever you wanted, *whenever* you wanted, to not have a care in the world, and to not have to worry about the ones you were leaving behind.

I sighed and decided I'd read one of the books Mr. Callahan had brought. My favorite place to read was outside, with my back tucked up against the tower where the sun had warmed the stone. I tiptoed inside to grab a book and peeked into the cradle. Panic blossomed like a rose in my chest. The cradle was empty.

"Celia?" I whirled, scanning the room. She couldn't have gone far. She wasn't even walking yet. I peeked under the table, then flew into the other rooms and checked under the beds. "Celia!" If she'd gone outside to find me, surely I would have seen her.

I leaped out the door. "Celia!" I ran around to the other side of the lighthouse, and a bitter taste, like iron, filled my mouth.

Celia was tottering toward the edge, swaying, arms outstretched to the sea. Beyond Celia, in the foam of the green waves, I saw two dark heads and knew what had drawn her to the cliffs. Seals.

I opened my mouth to scream her name but was afraid if I did, I might startle her and make her fall. I ran as I'd never run before.

Celia took another step. And then another.

I'd been so angry with her for ruining my life, resentful enough to even wish her gone. Be careful what you wish for, Mama had sometimes said.

Please, don't let her fall, I prayed. Let me reach her in time, and I'll never let her out of my sight again.

I was close enough now to hear her humming to herself, the sound she made whenever she saw seals, but already she was losing her balance, her chubby arms beginning to windmill, her mouth forming a little O of surprise.

I lunged and fell, sprawling hard on the rocks, and watched as Celia disappeared over the edge. But my outstretched hand caught the hem of her dress.

My arm felt like it had been pulled from its socket, but I held on and hauled Celia back up as though she were a fish on a line. Blood dripped from my chin and elbows, and Celia was shrieking, but I crushed her to my chest, shame and gratitude washing over me in equal measure. I would not let Celia out of my sight again.

CHAPTER ❧ 4

Mama had always said the best word to describe a good lighthouse keeper was *vigilant*, for they must be ever watchful and never let the light go out. But I became more vigilant than any lighthouse keeper, keeping Celia away from the cliff edge, watching out for things she could choke on or cut herself on. Whenever I felt the old resentment creeping in, I would play over in my mind the image of Celia disappearing over the cliff, and the anger would skulk away like a scolded dog and I'd hold Celia close. I was tired all the time, but even so, I knew Celia was a blessing. Her squeals of laughter and birdlike chatter kept the loneliness at bay and kept Papa and me from sinking into despair.

Papa helped me rig up a little harness for her, and when I was working around the house, I kept her tied to me with a rope so she wouldn't be able to sneak out without me. But I could tell Celia was as restless as I was, so before either of us got too snarlish, I'd take her out for a walk on the cliffs, with the rope like a leash. Celia could explore, but with her attached to me, I could let down my guard a little and enjoy our outings more. We'd carry out bread and toss it high for the seabirds, and watch their white wings flashing in sunlight as they snatched the bread out of the air, Celia clapping her hands and squealing, and I'd feel the closest thing to joy I'd felt since Mama died. When the bread was gone, we'd go to the far point of the island, where Celia would bark at the seals.

On stormy days, entertaining her was more of a challenge, but we'd read books and make up songs

(Celia wanted all songs to be about seals, of course), and I'd draw pictures of seals for her, and we'd play hide-and-seek. I let her help me knead bread dough and stir up cookies, and I told her everything I could remember about Mama.

I was both mother and sister to her and couldn't help but think how Mama would have loved her.

Sometimes, when I watched Celia twirling in the yard, bright-eyed, the sunlight catching her hair, I tried to imagine her parents. Celia had dark hair and startling green eyes, as pale as sea foam. Did she look like them? When she grew up, would her voice be like her mother's? Would she run like her father? We would never know who they were, but when Celia was old enough, I'd tell her about their brave, and seemingly desperate, attempt to save their daughter by lashing her between two mattresses as the ship was sinking. Whatever else we *didn't* know about them, Celia would always know that her parents had loved her.

I couldn't give Celia back her parents, but I'd make sure she never wanted for anything, including schooling.

"Just because there's no school on Devils Rock is no reason to grow up ignorant," Mama'd said. She'd ordered books, and a blackboard, and we'd spent hours each day memorizing multiplication tables and world capitals and reading Shakespeare and Longfellow. Longfellow was a favorite of Papa's, especially his poem "The Lighthouse":

> *And as the evening darkens, lo! how bright,*
> *Through the deep purple of the twilight air,*
> *Beams forth the sudden radiance of its light*
> *With strange, unearthly splendor in the glare!*
>
> *And the great ships sail outward and return,*
> *Bending and bowing o'er the billowy swells,*
> *And ever joyful, as they see it burn,*
> *They wave their silent welcomes and farewells,*

and Mama would recite "Twilight," one of her favorites. For the longest time I thought Mama had made that poem up about me for I often pressed my face against the window, peering out when storms lashed at our little light shining bravely into the night.

I was determined to do as good a job with Celia as Mama had done with me. I taught her the colors, and how to count to ten on her fingers, and she was learning the alphabet. Soon I'd get out Papa's maps and show her not only where our island rested off of Maine, but Africa and South America and China and the North Pole, so she'd know there was a world beyond our small island, places with mountains and rivers and prairies and trees.

The stories I'd loved most to hear were of Mama growing up on a farm. Mama told of milking cows, and making maple syrup, and picking apples in the fall. "Oh, Quila, you should have seen the trees," Mama said. "The apple trees are covered with snowy blossoms in the spring, and in the fall, the maple trees are the most beautiful shades of red and orange and gold." I tried to picture them in my mind, but I'd never seen a tree.

"You will," Mama said. "Someday I'll take you to meet your grandparents and uncles and aunts, and you'll get to climb trees." I was more excited to see the trees than the relatives. Mama and I had never gotten to see trees together, but maybe Celia and I would. I imagined her and me gathering sap in the spring to make the maple syrup, picking apples in the fall to make cider, and hiking through snowy woods to cut a balsam fir for Christmas.

I knew Celia wouldn't remember her first Christmas with us; she'd been too young, and with Papa and me still mourning Mama, we hadn't done much celebrating. But when our second Christmas with Celia rolled around, Papa and I were determined to make it something she'd never forget. Papa decorated the lighthouse with strings of dried apples and seashells, and carved Celia a seal from driftwood. I dug out Mama's recipes to fix the Scottish treats she'd always made for us: broonie, which was an oatmeal gingerbread, black bun fruitcake, and the pulled taffy that Mama called "Edinburgh rock." It was a difficult recipe, and I had to throw out the first two batches, but the third held together enough to pull. Celia ended up with taffy in her hair and eyelashes and even in her ears, and it took me two days to scrape pieces of candy from the floor and walls, but her laughter made it all worthwhile.

Spring came, with V's of geese winging north and clouds of seabirds coming back to Devils Rock. Celia and I spent hours watching the elegant gannets fold their wings and dive straight down into the sea for fish, and the comical little puffins bob like buoys on

the water. Looking at their brightly colored beaks, I laughed when I thought how Mama would have called them reefart-nosed, too.

We knew Celia had been born in the spring, but we didn't know the date, so Papa and I picked a day. I didn't want her to have to share a birthday with me, and we wanted to stay away from the date that Mama had died, so we chose May 15, for no particular reason other than that it seemed a good day for celebrating the end of winter.

I decided the occasion called for a cake, but cakes require eggs. Spring was just beginning, but I thought a few seabirds might have begun to nest. I rigged Celia up with her harness and rope and off we went to hunt for eggs.

I made her lie down beside me to peer over the cliff edge, and we did indeed spot a few eggs below us on the rock ledges. But how to get them? I couldn't take Celia with me when I climbed down for them, and I couldn't leave her at the top alone, because for certain she'd try and follow me; she'd already proven she was fearless. It was thinking about her adventuresome spirit that I hit upon a plan, one I was sure Papa would not approve of.

I checked the knots in the rope and made sure there were no frays along its entire length. Then I lowered Celia over the cliff edge until she could reach the eggs. I tried not to think about what Papa would say if he saw what we were doing, but Celia thought it great fun to dangle along the cliff face, picking eggs off their ledges, and begged for more when I pulled her up.

That summer, when Celia was two, we were housebound for four days by a monstrous storm that moaned and shrieked and pounded our little island. Papa hardly slept that whole time and kept the lamps burning, a beacon for any ships caught in the storm. I carried food and strong coffee up to him in the lantern room. Each time a wave crashed over the top of the tower, I felt the lighthouse shudder, and I was sure we would be washed away, just like the Minot's Ledge keepers. I wanted to spell Papa so he could catch a short nap, but the violence of the storm frightened Celia and she began to cry. I read her two books and had just put her to bed when Papa appeared in the doorway. He was dressed in his oilskins.

"A ship has run onto the shoals and is sinking," he said, his voice low. "I'm going out to see if I can rescue any on board."

He grabbed up a lantern, and I followed him outside. The wind tore at me, trying to spin me off my feet. Lightning flashed and, for an instant, I saw ship masts outlined against the sky. Above the roar of the storm, we could hear ship timbers groaning and cracking like kindling. Worse than that were the screams of the people on board.

I grabbed Papa's arm. "I'm going with you." But Papa shook off my hand.

"No, you have to stay here."

That made me angry.

"I'm not a child anymore, Papa," I said. "I'm strong. I can help."

"I know," Papa said. "It's Celia. . . ." He didn't finish his sentence, but he didn't have to. I understood. If anything should happen to Papa, there had to be someone to take care of Celia.

"Tend the light," Papa said. "The steamer will be by in a few weeks with more coal and supplies. If need be, you can go with them."

His words chilled me, more than the lashing rain and wind. The only reason for me to leave with the steamer would be if Papa didn't return.

Sick at heart, I watched Papa row away. His boat had never looked so tiny, the waves never so huge. They tossed his boat around as if it were a toy, and I knew I might never see Papa again.

evils Rock had never seemed so aptly named, for I felt surrounded by shrieking demons intent on tearing the world apart. The rock itself trembled as the waves slammed against it.

Staring out into the darkness, my mind racing, I thought the unthinkable.

What if something *did* happen to Papa? What if he didn't come back? I'd be an orphan, too, just like Celia. I'd have to wait for the steamer or a passing fisherman stopping by to take us off the island. But then where would we go? Who would we live with? I didn't know any of Papa's or Mama's family or how to find them. Could I raise Celia by myself?

Please let Papa be all right, I prayed.

With each flash of lightning, I could see the masts tilt more, until the flash when they were gone. There were no more screams, either.

I waited for what seemed like an hour, but Papa didn't return.

Soaked and shivering, I stumbled back into the lighthouse, crept into Celia's bed, and wrapped myself around her. I must have frightened her, for she woke, crying. So I rocked her in my lap, crooning, "It's all right. Everything will be all right," even after she'd fallen asleep again. I must have dozed myself, for the next thing I remember was hearing Papa shout, "Quila! Quick! Open the door!" and I leaped to do as he said, almost upsetting Celia onto the floor.

Papa came in like a gust of the storm, half carrying, half dragging a woman, her soaked skirts making a river on the floor.

"Help me, Quila," Papa gasped.

I grabbed her feet and helped lift her onto the bed.

"Strip off her wet things," Papa said. "I'm going to

heat some rocks in the fire. We'll pack them around her to try to warm her."

The woman's skin was blue, and she was ice-cold to the touch. Once I'd wrapped her in blankets, I rubbed her limbs to get her blood flowing. I talked to her the whole time, telling her she was safe now and begging her to wake up.

Papa lined the hot rocks alongside her body and poured little sips of hot tea between her lips, but most of it dribbled out the side. Both of us rubbed her legs and arms until I thought my arms would fall off.

She opened her eyes only once. They were green eyes, the color of the sea, but they were looking beyond me, to something I couldn't see. Her lips parted and I leaned forward to hear what she was trying to say.

"Mary?" she whispered. Her eyelids fluttered, then closed. A shudder ran through her body and she was gone.

CHAPTER 6

Debris from that shipwreck washed up against our island for days: broken beams, rope and sailcloth, lanterns, tin cups and a spoon, a family Bible with the name Barclay written inside, a doll that I washed and mended for Celia. Papa also found the bodies of two of the sailors, caught amongst the rocks.

There wasn't enough soil in the place where Papa had buried Mama and the woman to bury two more bodies, so Papa took them out in the boat, weighted the bodies down with rocks, and gave them back to the sea.

Papa hadn't talked much since Mama's death, and he grew even more silent after the wreck. He did his work without speaking, eating little and sleeping even less. I didn't sleep well, either. Each night I bolted awake from nightmares that had me tangled in ship's rigging, getting pulled into the darkness, icy water filling my lungs. I dreaded going to sleep, was afraid of the dreams that haunted me, but I tried to keep all that from Celia, and sang and played with her as if nothing had happened.

I led her carefully down the steep steps to where we could look for seashells and urchins in the tidal pools and where she could watch for seals. Celia refused to go to bed until she'd said good night to them.

"Boat toming," Celia sang.

Startled, I lifted my head. I hadn't seen anything when we'd first come outside. It was unlike me to miss anything on the horizon, but a few moments later I saw she was right, there was a boat approaching. It was a rowboat, like Papa's, and I watched the rhythm of the oars dipping into the water.

"It's Mr. Richardson," I said. "But there's someone with him."

We watched as Mr. Richardson drew closer, until we could see his passenger was a woman.

The boat scraped against the rocks. Mr. Richardson jumped into the shallow water and steadied the boat while the woman stepped out. She held her skirts up and waded to shore.

"Hello," she said.

I was tongue-tied, not used to strangers. But Celia piped right up.

"See my dolly?" she said, holding up the doll from the shipwreck.

The woman smiled.

"What a precious child," she said. She talked with such a thick accent I could scarcely understand her. She looked at me, and I saw blue eyes, so blue they could have been snipped from the sky. Mama's eyes had been more like the blue of the sea.

"Are you the keeper here?" she asked.

She knew how to win my heart, pretending to mistake me for the keeper. I smiled back.

"No, my papa is," I said. "He's up in the lantern room right now."

"Well, I guess it's him I should be talking to, then,

to see if I could have lodging here for a day or two, until my business is done."

What possible business could she have here? I wondered, but I knew it wasn't polite to ask.

Papa came down the stairs from the tower just then, wiping soot from his hands. He'd been polishing the reflectors. He was startled to see an unfamiliar face.

"May I help you?"

"Mr. MacKinnon, my name is Margaret Malone. I'm here to say goodbye to my sister."

I could see by the look on Papa's face he was as puzzled as I was.

There were tears in Margaret Malone's eyes as she spoke.

"My sister went down in a shipwreck somewhere off this island and I've come to say my goodbyes."

CHAPTER 7

It took a few moments for Papa to find his voice.

"It's poor hosts we are, keeping you standing out here. You must be hungry. As for staying here, you can take Aquila's room. She'll sleep with Celia."

When Miss Malone tried to protest, Papa waved his hand.

"You'll be doing us a favor, Miss Malone, bringing us news from the outside. We get so few visitors here. I only worry my girls may tire you out with all their questions."

Miss Malone smiled at me.

"I shall enjoy their company," she said.

"Quila, show Miss Malone where she can put her bag, and you might as well give her a tour of the place," Papa said.

I was near to bursting with wanting to ask Miss Malone about her sister, but I did as Papa said.

There wasn't much to give a tour of, the kitchen, three bedrooms above that, and the lantern room at the top, but I did my best. Miss Malone had all sorts of questions about how we lived, and what we did, and how we cared for the light, and she marveled at the way the cupboards and sink and beds were built into the circular walls, saying she'd never thought of lighthouse rooms being *round*. I'd never thought of rooms as being anything *but* round, and Miss Malone laughed when I told her this.

We'd lost track of time, and Papa had to remind me about supper. I hustled about fixing cornbread with codfish gravy.

"This gravy is as fine as my mum used to make, the few times we had cod to eat," Miss Malone said. "You're a fine cook, Aquila."

"Thank you, Miss Malone."

"Oh, please call me Margaret."

Papa was always hungry for news.

"Which candidate do you favor in the coming election?" he asked. "I like what I hear about that young lawyer from Illinois, Abe Lincoln, but I fear the country will go to war if he's elected."

Margaret looked surprised.

"There's not many men who'll ask a woman's opinion on politics," she said. "Are you for women having the vote?"

Papa looked thoughtful.

"Why, yes, I am," he said, and I felt proud. Mama said Papa was a "forward thinker."

With Margaret there, dinner seemed like a party. Celia clapped her hands and sang a song about seals that I'd taught her. Margaret stared at her in astonishment.

"My mother taught me that song when I was a girl," she said.

"Celia loves seals," I said. "She talks to them. There's usually one waiting for her every morning down off the point." I didn't mention the day she'd almost fallen from the cliffs, for that is something I had not told Papa, either.

"My sister loved seals, too," Margaret said softly. "We lived two days' walk from the sea, so we didn't get there often, but when we did, my sister would sing that song for the seals and they'd gather round her. I think she would have gone with them, if she could. My da said it was because she was black Irish."

"What's black Irish?" I asked.

"My mother, father, and me had blue eyes and fair skin that burns easily in the sun, but my sister had black hair and green eyes. The old folk say that once upon a time, fishermen married seals, and children with that blood in them are dark-haired, and wild, and drawn to the sea." Margaret giggled. "Whenever Da told that story, Mum would slap him and say, '*I'm* not a seal! It must be from *your* side of the family!'"

"So, you're from Ireland?" I asked.

"Quila," Papa scolded. "Let the woman eat." But Margaret just smiled.

"She's just curious is all, as I'm sure all of you are, about my sister and what brought me here," Margaret said. "You've been so kind. 'Tis only fair that I tell you my story."

I hadn't had someone tell me stories since Mama

died, and it brought tears to my eyes remembering all the evenings she sat on my bed, spinning tales of Knights of the Round Table and Arabian Nights, of snow-covered mountains and steamy jungles and oceans of grass. Mama's stories were so vivid, I could see it all in my mind: tigers and monkeys and green parrots in the jungle, wild horses racing over prairies.

"Yes, I'm from Ireland," Margaret said. "County Galway. Times were hard enough, but it's all we'd ever known, hard times, and we got by until the Great Hunger, the potato blight. The potatoes turned black in the fields. There was no food, no money to pay rents, and the English turned us out of our homes. My parents didn't have much but they sold everything they had. It would have fed us all, for a little while. But when that food was gone, there would have been no hope for any of us, so my parents saw it as a chance to save one of us. There was enough money to buy a ticket, enough to send one of us to America. My mother said I should go, as my sister was too young, so I sailed away from the only home I'd ever known, away from my family, knowing I might never see them again.

"I found work in the woolen mills in Lawrence, Massachusetts. Word came a few months later that my parents had died of the hunger and my sister was living with an aunt who didn't want another mouth to feed. I worked in the mills, on the looms, for ten years, saving every cent so that I could send for my sister. When I sent her the money, she wrote to me telling me she had married, so I borrowed money and sent it so both of them could come. She put off the trip again, as she was expecting, but after the baby was born, the three of them set sail for New York. They never arrived. They were caught in a terrible storm and lost at sea somewhere off the coast of Maine."

Margaret's voice broke, but I hardly noticed as a shiver ran through me.

"She was here," I said. "Your sister was here."

"Now, Quila," Papa said, "we don't know if that woman was—" But I interrupted him.

"It was her, I know it was."

Margaret stared at me, wide-eyed.

"Your sister," I repeated. "Papa rescued her. We saw the ship going down and Papa rowed out to help them, and he did save a woman. He brought her back but she only lived a little while. She had dark hair and green eyes."

Margaret was crying now, silent sobs that shook her body.

"The baby?" she choked.

Papa shook his head.

"I'm sorry, no, I didn't see a baby. By the time I rowed out, the ship had broken up and I found her floating in the debris. I wish I could have saved her. I'm sorry."

"You did all you could," Margaret said. "I'm the one to blame. If I hadn't sent for her, she'd still be alive. Now I have no one left."

I knew about loss and emptiness.

"Papa buried her next to Mama," I said gently. "When you're up to it, I'll show you."

Margaret nodded, her eyes closed.

"I think I'll rest awhile," she said. I showed her to my bed and tried to keep Celia quiet. I read her a book, but she wiggled out of my lap. I cut out some paper dolls for her, but Celia wanted to bang on pots instead. I got some string and was showing Celia how to play cat's cradle when Margaret reappeared in the doorway. Her eyes were red and swollen and I was sure she hadn't gotten any sleep.

"I'll make you some tea," I said. "Mama said things always look better after a cup of tea."

"My mother said the same thing," Margaret said. "Two wise women. You must miss her terribly."

I ducked my head so Margaret wouldn't see the tears that sprang to my eyes, and nodded. While I made tea, Margaret took the same string we'd played cat's cradle with and looped a button onto it. She twirled the button between her hands, winding up the string, and when she pulled on the string, the button whirled like a top, making a buzzing sound. Celia squealed with delight.

Margaret drank her tea slowly, and sighed.

"Your mum was right, I do feel better. I think I'm ready to have you show me where my sister is buried."

I'd visited Mama's grave every day since she'd died. I'd tried planting flowers but nothing had taken root, so I kept the area swept clean. Clods of dirt and rocks marked the fresh grave Papa had dug. When I saw the look on Margaret's face, I was ashamed I hadn't yet raked and smoothed out her sister's grave.

"I'll take better care of it," I promised.

"I don't understand," Margaret said. "This is a fresh grave."

The shock must have been too much for her, I thought, so I tried to be as gentle as I could.

"Yes, Papa buried her ten days ago."

"Oh, no," Margaret said. "You must be mistaken. The ship my sister was on went down two years ago."

CHAPTER ❧ 8

Margaret went to bed early, exhausted. Papa and I huddled next to the stove, whispering.

"We have to tell her," Papa said.

I wanted to weep.

"She'll take Celia away," I said.

Papa looked ready to weep, too, but he was firm.

"I know," he said. "But we have to tell her. She has no one else. She has to know she has a niece." He stood up.

"There's a storm brewing and I must go up to light the lamps, but we'll tell her in the morning."

He climbed the stairs of the tower and I knew he thought the matter was settled. But I wasn't going to sit still and let Margaret cart off Celia without a fight. As bad as I felt for Margaret, I couldn't be as unselfish as Papa. Celia had saved Papa and me. Losing her would be as bad as losing Mama. I couldn't go through that again.

Celia opened her eyes when I picked her up.

"Where we doning?" she murmured.

"On a trip," I told her. She nodded and closed her eyes again.

I didn't dare light a lantern for fear Papa would see us, so I stumbled down the stone steps with only the moon to guide me, feeling each step with my foot before I put my weight on it.

It took all my strength to drag Papa's boat to the water's edge. I wrapped Celia in an oilskin and settled her into the bow. There was a strong wind blowing as I pushed off. Luckily, it was blowing toward the mainland, for I was sure I never would have been able to row against it. That wind smelled of bad weather ahead. I hoped I could outrun the storm and reach the mainland before it hit.

I'd never rowed Papa's skiff before and hadn't known how hard it would be. Papa made it look effortless, but I couldn't keep it going straight. It pulled to either one side or the other, sometimes one oar out of the water when the other was in. The beacon from our light gleamed brightly, a comfort in the darkness. In all my fourteen years at Devils Rock, I'd never seen the light from the water. I thought of Papa up in the lantern room, keeping his vigil, thinking we were safely asleep in our room. I hoped someday he'd understand why I'd done this and forgive me.

I rowed and rowed and rowed and it seemed I hadn't moved an inch. How would I ever reach the mainland at this rate?

I braced my feet and yanked hard on the oars. They came out of the water fast and I fell backward off the seat into the few inches of water sloshing about in the bottom of the boat. The boat lurched to one side and I just managed to grab Celia before she slid into the sea. I settled her back into the bow and sat down, soaked and sobered. I'd almost tipped us over. I had to be more careful.

The moon made a path on the water, and I rowed

along that silver river. A dark shape bobbed behind us on the moon path, went under, and popped up again. A seal was following us, no doubt curious about what we were doing. Maybe it was one of Celia's seals that always seemed to be watching for her. Seeing its dark head cheered me and I felt less alone.

The night wore on and the storm clouds gathered, hiding the moon. The wind blew fiercer, and colder, and the waves grew higher, tossing our little boat around like a cork. Water sloshed in over the gunwales. We had oilskins on, but still it was terribly cold and Celia began to whimper.

"Hush now," I said, "we'll be there soon." But in truth, the pinpoints of light on the far shore, lanterns gleaming from windows, weren't getting any closer, and I was tired, so tired.

I let go of the oars and picked Celia up, tucking her inside my coat as best I could, thinking that would protect her from the wind and warm her. The wind spun the boat sideways and the next wave caught us broadside, flipping us over.

I gasped as the shock of the icy water hit me, and salt water filled my nose, mouth, and lungs. I flailed with my arms and legs, trying to escape the water, to get air, and my head broke the surface for a moment. I choked and vomited, and another wave hit me, driving me under. Celia was struggling inside my coat, kicking and gurgling.

So this is what it's like to drown, I thought, and I was ashamed for bringing Celia to this. Her parents' love had saved her once. My selfishness was going to kill her.

Lights exploded in my head and I heard a voice. It was Mama's voice.

"Quila," she said, "remember the orange?"

Once, for no other reason than that he was lonely, a ship's captain had anchored off our island and spent the evening with us, dazzling us with tales of his travels in the South Seas and around the Horn. As he was leaving, he'd held out his hand to me. In his palm was an orange ball.

"For your girl," he said to Mama, smiling.

I just stared at the object in his hand, not knowing what it was but knowing I wanted it.

"You may take it, Quila," Mama said gently, and I'd lifted it from his palm as if it were made of glass.

Mama took a knife and peeled off the outer layer, revealing a smaller ball inside. Mama pulled pieces off the ball, and I began to cry, thinking she'd broken my gift from the captain.

Mama held one of the pieces toward me.

"Taste it," she said.

I bit into it gingerly, and sweet, tangy juice flooded my mouth.

I was so startled I sat down, and Mama burst out laughing.

"It's an orange," she said.

It was rare that we ever saw fruits or vegetables on our table. Mama had tried growing a few vegetables in the only patch of soil the island possessed, but with the bruising winds and punishing salt spray, all that survived were a few lettuce leaves and a radish or two.

I ate the orange slowly, savoring each bite, and licked my fingers when it was gone. Nothing before or since has ever tasted as wonderful as that orange, and the thought now came to my mind: Celia would never get to taste an orange.

I heard a voice again and saw a figure ahead, and I tried to call out, Mama, wait, come back, help me, but

the sea was in my mouth and lungs and I couldn't speak, I couldn't breathe, and I was sinking down, down to where the fishes would feast on my bones. The figure turned its head and I saw it wasn't Mama at all, but a woman with dark hair and green eyes.

Something slammed into me, something solid but alive, and then it was several bodies, all of them sleek and slippery, moving first beside me, then beneath, lifting me up. I stopped struggling and let myself be borne along.

CHAPTER ❧ 9

Mr. Richardson often told the story afterward of how he'd gone down to the pier and found Celia and me on the beach. At first he thought we were clumps of seaweed and was pushing off in his boat when Celia whimpered. Both of us were half-frozen and bruised, and Celia had a cut over one eye, but we were alive and none too worse for wear.

He took us to his house, and his wife fussed over us, wrapping us in blankets while she dried our clothes by the fire and feeding us tea and honey, but neither of us could stop shivering. My teeth chattered against the rim of Mrs. Richardson's china cup.

"As soon as you've warmed up, I'll take you home," Mr. Richardson said.

Mrs. Richardson glared at him.

"You'll not be taking them off to sea again today," she said firmly. "After what they've been through."

"But I have to, Bet," Mr. Richardson said. "Imagine their father thinking them lost for good." So Mrs. Richardson finally relented, though she hugged us so hard when we said our goodbyes I thought poor Celia's eyes would pop from her head.

While Mr. Richardson rowed us home, I told him about the seals carrying Celia and me to shore.

"You'll not be wanting to tell that story to too many folk, or they'll think you're daft," Mr. Richardson said, "but I believe you. You can't spend a life at sea like I have and not see some strange happenings."

It was a bittersweet voyage home. I was glad I was alive and glad I hadn't killed Celia, but I dreaded going back. For sure Margaret would take Celia now.

Papa looked like he'd aged twenty years, and he was shaking when he grabbed us up in a bear hug.

Margaret should have been furious with me, but she hugged me, too.

"I'm so glad you're both all right."

I could hardly look her in the eye. "I need to tell you something."

"Your father already told me," Margaret said, and I hung my head, but she squeezed my shoulder.

"I would have done the same thing," she said. "Nothing's more important than family, don't you think?" There were tears in Margaret's eyes and I realized with Celia gone, I'd still have Papa, no matter how brokenhearted we'd be. But without Celia, Margaret would have no one.

"What are you going to do, now that you know?" I asked.

"I don't know," Margaret said. "But would it be all right if I stayed on a little longer, get to know Celia better, and think about what I want to do?"

I squeezed Celia tight and couldn't speak.

"Yes," Papa said. "You're welcome to stay as long as you like."

"When I do leave, I can't ask you to leave the light unattended to get me to the mainland," Margaret said. "Is there any other way off the island?"

"There's Mr. Callahan, the lighthouse inspector," Papa said. "He comes by about every six months or so."

"Fine," Margaret said, relieved. "I'll stay until Mr. Callahan comes."

CHAPTER ⋄ 10

e spent the next weeks getting to know each other.

I came to question Papa's decision to let Margaret stay, thinking it might have been easier if Margaret had just taken Celia away then and there instead of prolonging the agony of having her ripped from our lives. I found myself watching Celia, study-ing her, trying to memorize every detail of her, know-ing that when Margaret took her away, memories would be all I'd have left. When I thought of what life on the island would be like without Celia, just Papa and me rattling around in the lighthouse, I pictured my heart falling apart in sections, like that orange.

Margaret didn't look strong, but she was a good worker, and she did her share around the lighthouse, work that Mama had often done: cleaning the copper and brass fixtures, sweeping the tower stairway, and keeping the lantern room clean and dusted. One day I caught her sprinkling salt over Celia while she slept.

"It's to keep the fairies from stealing her," Margaret explained. According to her, the fairy people spent most of their time feasting, fighting, and playing beautiful music, but would keep misfortune from your door if you left them a bowl of milk on the doorstep each evening. Which she did.

Each day, when our work was done, Celia and I showed Margaret our island: the nesting sites where we gathered eggs, the tidal pools where we collected shells, the tiny wildflowers nestled in the rocks. Sometimes Celia would reach up to hold Margaret's hand, and it twisted my heart to see it, but I knew I didn't have to worry about Celia's future. Margaret would take good care of her, of that I was certain.

Margaret was cheerful, willing to jump in and help with what had to be done, her laughter like sunshine

after a storm, someone Mama would have loved. Perhaps that's why I disliked her. What right did she have to be cheerful when she was going to break our hearts again by taking away Celia? What right did she have to act like part of the family when she was going to tear it apart? I resented the way she'd slipped into the hole left by Mama, as if she belonged, as if she could take Mama's place.

There were little agonies every day—watching Margaret stir up cornbread in Mama's blue china bowl, using Mama's sewing kit to mend Papa's pants (even squinting the same way to thread the needle)—and it was worse because Papa didn't seem to notice the way she was wiggling into his heart, pushing out Mama.

I first noticed it when we painted the lighthouse. Papa had waited for a mild day, with little wind, and Margaret and I painted up as high as we could reach while Papa did all the high work, dangling from a rope out of the lantern room. Even Celia helped, or tried to, and Papa pretended to scold all of us, saying we'd gotten more paint on ourselves than we had on the lighthouse. Margaret looked down with dismay at her dress to discover it was true.

"You can tear it up for rags," Papa said.

"That's easy for you to say," Margaret said, "but I didn't bring much with me when I came here, since I wasn't planning on staying long. But I wouldn't expect a man to notice such things."

I hadn't noticed, either, being that I didn't pay much attention to clothes. Secretly, I'd always longed to wear pants, to be able to run and climb and not have to worry about silly petticoats, or being ladylike, though I'd never quite dared admit that to Mama.

"I'll just have to wear it, paint and all," Margaret said. "I can always say it's the latest rage." But I could tell Papa felt bad.

"I guess Marion's clothes would fit you," he said slowly. "You go on in and help yourself to what you need."

For just a moment, I stopped breathing. Mama's clothes had sat untouched in her wardrobe since she'd died, except for the times I'd buried my nose in them, the smell of her bringing her face to mind. Every day, I tried to remember her exactly as she'd been, though now the face was blurry, like a photograph where someone has moved. It scared me that Papa was pushing his memories of her out of his life, the way you put away clothes you've grown out of.

"Oh, I couldn't," Margaret said, glancing at me. "It wouldn't be right." But Papa shook his head.

"Those dresses and things are just going to waste," he said, "and Quila won't want them."

My eyes stung. Papa hadn't even asked me whether I wanted Mama's clothes or not, but even if I didn't want them, I didn't want to see Margaret in them.

I was afraid Margaret would select Mama's pretty green delaine, the one she wore at holidays, but she picked the most worn of Mama's dresses, a faded yellow calico that Mama had already patched once. Still, it was a shock to look up and see Mama's dress without Mama in it.

I think it was Mama's dress that made Papa start noticing Margaret. She and I were doing the laundry, and Margaret, little as she was, was struggling with carrying the water from the cistern. Papa lugged the pails for her, then carried the basket to the clothesline, where I pegged up the wet clothes.

"You never helped Mama with the laundry," I said, more sharply than I meant to.

"Your mother didn't need help," Papa said. "She was strong. Margaret's not like her."

No, she's not, I wanted to shout, but bit my lip and pulled another sheet from the basket. The wind tried to tear it from my hands, so Papa grabbed one end and held it until I could get both corners pegged tight.

"When did you get so tall?" he asked. He was frowning, looking at me like he hadn't seen me for a long time. "You look just like your mother."

I'm ashamed to admit that my heart sank at his words. I'd loved Mama with all my heart, but she'd said herself she was as plain as a hedge fence. I'd never seen a hedge, or a fence, either one, but I knew it wasn't a compliment. Mama's beauty was inside.

Papa smiled, not knowing the thoughts in my head.

"As pretty as the day I met her," he added.

I sighed.

"Mama wasn't pretty, Papa," I said.

Papa looked like I'd slapped him.

"She was to me," he said. In that moment, I forgave him everything.

Or I thought I had until he started lingering over his breakfast tea, telling Margaret stories of his childhood at sea: of stowing away on a ship to Singapore, of being shipwrecked on an island for three weeks with nothing to eat but coconuts, of seeing icebergs and polar bears in the North Sea and coral reefs and rainbow-colored fish in the warm waters of the Southern Hemisphere. I stared at him in astonishment, for I could scarcely believe those stories were true. All those years of hearing Mama's stories—and even the past two years with Celia, when I'd tried to remember every story I'd ever heard and made up a great many, to keep Celia happy—he'd never breathed a word about his childhood, never let on that he'd had one great adventure after another. It was like meeting a stranger, like watching Rip Van Winkle emerge from his twenty-year sleep, except Papa seemed almost boyish, lighthearted, with something that had been missing in him since Mama died. And it was Margaret that was bringing that out in him, not me.

"I didn't know your father was such a storyteller," Margaret said.

Neither did I, I thought bitterly.

Margaret was a good storyteller, too, almost as good at weaving tales as Mama had been, and though

I pretended not to care for Margaret's stories, I always sat close enough to hear her tell of Grace O'Malley, the Irish queen who was a sea pirate. Mama had told me about Blackbeard, but I'd never heard of a woman pirate before.

"She even stole a baby," Margaret said. "She'd come ashore to get supplies of food and water for her ship, and stopped at Howth Castle. The family was eating and wouldn't let her in. Grace was so angry, she stole their son and sailed away with him. She only returned the boy when Lord Howth promised to keep the castle gates open at mealtimes and to always set a place at the head of the table for the head of the O'Malley clan."

Papa laughed, again something I'd not seen from him since Mama died, but I couldn't help thinking that Margaret was a bit of a pirate herself, for soon she'd be stealing Celia away from us.

It wasn't the only thing she was taking, for when I looked next in Mama's wardrobe, three more of her dresses were missing, including the green delaine. I didn't mention it to Papa; he'd told her she could have them. But it seemed like stealing to me.

I started to let go of Celia, preparing myself for the day she would leave. I was less patient, snapping at her when she climbed into my lap wanting a story. "I don't have time for you right now. Have Margaret read to you." Her green eyes would well up with tears, and I'd have to turn away so she wouldn't see my own.

At the same time I was pushing her away, I found it harder and harder to see Margaret and Celia together, the way Margaret rested her hand on Celia's head or licked her finger to clean a smudge off Celia's cheek, the way Celia would snuggle her head under Margaret's chin when she was tired. But once, when I suggested that Margaret take Celia out alone to explore, Margaret looked at me and slowly shook her head.

"Oh, Aquila, you're as dear to me as she is," she said softly, and my breath caught ragged in my throat. I'd had a father, mother, and sister, but I'd never had a friend before. I felt guilty for thinking such bad thoughts of her, but I was sad, too. In any other circumstances, we might have been friends.

Nights were long, as sleep did not come easily for me, and I'd slip out to sit on the cliffs, listening to the wind and the groaning sea, and think "if onlys." If only

Papa had taken Mama to the doctor. If only Margaret hadn't come to Devils Rock. If only the ship her sister was on had not gone down. . . . But here I had to stop, for without that shipwreck, we would never have known Celia. It was going to be heart-wrenching to lose her, but I could not imagine those two years without her.

Some nights I'd hear wild geese, too, hurrying south. I thought of Margaret and how she'd soon be moving on, too, like the geese, before the cold set in. Never before had I dreaded a winter on Devils Rock as I did now.

On one of those nights, I rose from the rocks, stiff from the damp chill, and climbed the hill to say good night to Mama. Margaret and I startled each other. She stood silhouetted against the sky, her face bathed in moonlight.

"I miss my sister on nights like this especially," she said. "Our mum told us the fairies lived in the Land of Light but the door to their land was open only on nights when the moon was full. It was said that if a piece of metal shaped by human hands was put in the doorway to their land, the door could not close, so on moonlit nights, my sister and I stood on the hill near our home with a horseshoe, waiting for the door to open. I guess I'm still waiting."

Times like that, it was hard to hate her. That, and when she was singing.

Margaret sang even more than Mama had. She taught Celia Irish lullabies she'd heard her mum sing, and she taught Papa and me some shanty Irish songs she'd learned from her da. Music was as natural to Margaret as breathing. Often I saw Papa pause on the stairs or in the doorway, listening to her, and once he asked her the name of the tune she was humming.

"'Lovely Leitrim,'" Margaret answered, and sang:

> *Last night I had a pleasant dream.*
> *I woke up with a smile.*
> *I dreamed that I was back again*
> *in dear old Erin's Isle.*
> *In all the lands that I have been,*
> *throughout the East and West,*
> *In all the lands that I have seen,*
> *I love my own the best.*

Papa didn't say anything, but later, as he climbed the steps to light the lamps, I heard him humming it to himself.

Margaret and I were cleaning the clutter from the closet when she found the fiddle case.

"Does your da play?" she asked.

"He did," I said. "But not since Mama died."

"'Tis a shame," Margaret said, "for a fiddle's meant to be played. I could teach you the Irish jig." I remembered the joy I'd felt when Mama twirled me around the floor and the words flew out of my mouth before I could snatch them back.

"Couldn't you show me anyway?" I begged, and Margaret laughed.

"Sure, and why not," she said. "To dance, you only need music in your heart."

Margaret clapped and sang while I shuffled across the floor, but my feet felt as clumsy as rocks. I decided I must not have a musical heart.

"Nothing comes easy at first," Margaret said. "It just takes practice."

Each morning, we'd wait until Papa had gone out to check storm damage on the boat landing, or climbed the tower to polish the reflectors, and we'd push back the table and chairs to make room. Celia loved the dance lessons, and she'd stand on my feet while I skipped from side to side. Sometimes all three of us held hands and spun in wild circles till we were too dizzy to stand.

Margaret was calling out the steps of a new dance one morning, and so focused was I on my feet that I didn't realize she'd stopped singing. I looked up and caught my breath. Papa stood in the doorway, holding his fiddle.

He lifted it to his chin and played "Lovely Leitrim" as if he'd practiced it for years. Margaret looked like she was going to burst into tears. Then Papa played "Aura Lee" and "Barbara Allen" and "Lorena," all sad tunes, and his fiddle spoke of such heartbreak and longing that I was sure Mama must be crying in heaven.

Papa finished and looked at our faces.

"If Marion were here, she'd say, 'Goodness, Franklin, play something cheerful!' Isn't that right, Quila?" And I nodded. That did sound like Mama.

"We need a dance tune," Papa said, and lit into "Highland Laddie." I grabbed Celia's hands and we hopped and skipped and slid across the floor, Celia shrieking with laughter. Papa played "The Fairy Dance" and "Blue Bonnets over the Border" till Celia and I collapsed.

Margaret put her hands on her hips and gave a nod to Papa. He played "Lark in the Morning" and "Paddy's Leather Breeches" while she jigged round the kitchen, the click of her feet sounding like stones washing against the shore, faster and faster, until the door flew open and she fell into Mr. Callahan's arms.

Papa's fiddle stopped in mid-tune, and the music and laughter died away. All my preparations for this day, the way I'd steeled myself against losing Celia, disappeared, too.

For weeks, the question of when Margaret would leave had been like an elephant in the parlor: it was on everyone's mind, even if no one mentioned it. But we hadn't been expecting Mr. Callahan for months yet, thought we had lots more time. Now the elephant had trumpeted its way into our living room, for Mr. Callahan had arrived early.

"You must be the lovely lass Mr. Richardson told me about. I understand I'm to transport you down to Boston," Mr. Callahan said.

All this time I thought I'd been preparing myself for Margaret to leave, too, had thought I'd be glad to see her go, and I found I wasn't prepared at all. I could no more imagine a day without seeing Margaret than I could a life without Celia.

Margaret looked at Papa as if she expected him to say something. He was looking at her as if he expected her to say something.

I was watching them both. I could see Papa's jaw muscles working; he was turning over something in his mind, but there wasn't any sound coming out of his mouth.

All he had to say was "I hope you'll stay awhile longer." But he didn't.

I looked at Margaret. All she had to say was "No, thank you, Mr. Callahan. I've decided I won't be leaving just yet." But she didn't.

Looking back, I can recognize that they were two wounded souls who were afraid to love again. But I was too young to understand it then.

Papa was the first to drop his eyes, so perhaps I'm the only one who noticed Margaret's shoulders droop, or how her voice came out flat and listless when she spoke.

"Thank you, Mr. Callahan, that would be most kind of you. I'll pack my things after supper, and be ready to go first thing in the morning."

Margaret put apples to soak and mixed piecrust while I pared potatoes and stirred up biscuits. While we ate, Mr. Callahan told Margaret the story of Abby Burgess, and told me that the Lighthouse Board (and Abby, too) was quite enthusiastic about my idea of a lighthouse library, but I hardly heard him. Mr. Callahan was here, and Margaret would be leaving with him in the morning, taking Celia with her.

Mr. Callahan tried to entertain us at supper, but when he saw no one was listening, he stopped talking and just ate. It was so quiet we could hear him chewing. As for the rest of us, our food sat untouched on our plates. Celia didn't understand what was going on, but she knew things were not right, and kept looking from one to the other, a puzzled expression on her face.

As soon as Mr. Callahan finished, Margaret stood to clear the table.

"Quila, would you help me get Celia's things together?" she said.

I followed her into the room Celia and I shared and watched as she began to pull things out of the dresser: Celia's dresses, stockings, her woolen coat and hat.

I didn't say anything because I could feel the sting of tears in the back of my throat and knew if I started crying, I wouldn't be able to stop. It wasn't until Margaret picked up Celia's driftwood seal and her doll that we realized Celia had followed us.

"What you duning?" she asked, and it came to me we hadn't prepared Celia at all for what was about to happen. She had no idea she was leaving us. I swallowed hard and crouched in front of her.

"You're going on a trip," I told her, trying to sound as cheerful as I could. "You're going on a trip with Margaret."

Celia frowned.

"Go smimming with Marget?" she said. I puzzled over her words until I realized the only time Celia had heard the word *trip* was when I'd run off with her and ended up almost drowning her. No wonder she was suspicious.

"No, honey, a good trip. No swimming." I pulled her to me, and my arms ached when I realized this would be the last time I'd ever hold her. I felt sick at the thought of losing her, but I was also envious of all she would see and experience. Margaret had told us some about her life in Lawrence, about the mills and board-inghouses, the lectures and concerts that she and the other mill girls attended at night. Someday I'd see the sights that Celia was about to see, know what it was like to ride in a carriage down a street lit with lamps, listen to an orchestra play, sit in a library and know that every book there was just waiting for me to read it.

"I'm sure some of her things are in my room, too," Margaret said. "Your room," she corrected herself. "You'll probably be glad to get it back." But I didn't feel glad, even after I followed Margaret into her room and saw, draped over the back of the chair, the dresses I'd noticed missing from Mama's wardrobe: the blue print, the red calico, and the green delaine. What I felt was anger, white-hot anger that boiled up in me like a storm-tossed sea. Isn't it enough that you're taking Celia? I wanted to shout. Do you have to take Mama's dresses, too? Margaret wasn't even trying to hide them. In fact, she scooped them up and held them out to me.

"I took them in and shortened the hems," she said. "The green should look especially good on you."

Shame flooded over me, putting out the fire of my

anger. She hadn't stolen them at all. She'd altered them to fit me.

"Thank you for being my friend," Margaret said, and I saw she was fighting back tears. "It's not everyone that gets to experience life in a lighthouse, and to have such a good teacher."

I wanted to slink away, like a dog with its tail between its legs. I'd treated her horribly. I hadn't been a friend to her at all. But she had been one to me, and now I was losing her, too. Why was it that whenever I loved someone, they were taken from me? First Mama, and now Celia and Margaret.

"Margaret?" Papa's voice startled us both. He'd come to the doorway, but seemed afraid to come in. "There's something I'd like to ask you."

Margaret turned toward him, and I could see she was holding her breath.

"I want you to take Quila with you," he said.

It wasn't the question she'd been expecting and it caught her off guard. It caught me off guard, too. Papa was sending me away?

"She could tend to Celia while you're at work in the mills," Papa went on, "and then in the evenings go to some of those lectures and concerts you've talked about."

"Quila's welcome to come with me," Margaret said, keeping her voice even. "But have you asked her what she wants? She's not a child anymore."

"I know that," Papa said. "That's why she should go with you. She needs a woman's influence. She needs more than I can give her."

Papa walked away, so he didn't hear Margaret's answer.

"You mean she needs more than you're willing to give," she said. I did hear her, but I didn't understand what she meant.

CHAPTER 11

I slept not one wink that night. I felt like a ship dashed on the rocks, with the sea pushing me one way, and the wind pulling me another. How could I decide between staying and leaving, between living with Papa or abandoning him to go with Margaret and Celia? There was the lure of faraway places, and my love of Devils Rock, both of them strong and tugging at me.

Not having slept, I rose early to fix breakfast. Margaret stumbled in and I could tell that she hadn't slept, either. Neither of us was hungry again, so Mr. Callahan got three servings of porridge, and I kept Papa's hot on the back of the stove. But Papa didn't come for breakfast.

I knocked on his door. When there was no answer, I peeked in. His bed hadn't been slept in. I checked the tower. The lamps were still burning. Papa had not been in the tower room. With fear beginning to prickle my skin, I ran down to the boat landing. Papa's skiff was gone.

Papa had never left like that before. Something was terribly wrong.

Margaret was as worried as I was.

"Why would he just leave without telling us?" she said.

"I'm sure there's no need to worry," Mr. Callahan said. "He probably just went for supplies."

"He would have told us," Margaret said.

Mr. Callahan frowned. "Has Mr. MacKinnon ever left the light unattended before?" he asked.

Margaret whirled on him, and I swear her eyes were snapping blue sparks.

"The light is *not* unattended," she said. "Quila is here and she's every bit as capable of keeping the light as Mr. MacKinnon or Abby Burgess or anyone else, for that matter!"

I smiled, thinking Abby just might have met her

match in Margaret Malone, and I was grateful for Margaret's loyalty, but worried no less.

"I guess I can wait here one more day," Mr. Callahan said, "but I'll have to leave tomorrow. If Mr. MacKinnon hasn't returned by then, I'll have to appoint a replacement."

I blew out the lamps, trimmed the wicks, and polished the reflectors. I was grateful I had something to keep my hands busy, but wished the same for my mind. I couldn't come up with a good reason for Papa to leave the way he had, and worried about his state of mind. His heart had never healed from losing Mama, and to lose Margaret, too . . . maybe he'd left us for good. If that were true, and if Margaret left with Celia, I'd be truly alone. I could see myself roaming the cliffs at night, my hair wild, keening into the wind, growing mad as Mrs. Blair had.

I spent the day on the cliffs, my eyes trained on the horizon, watching for Papa's boat, but there was nothing but the grey sea.

Margaret brought out a woolen blanket and wrapped it around my shoulders.

"Come in for some hot tea," she said, but I shook my head.

"He'll be all right," Margaret said. "If ever a man could take care of himself, it's your father." She hesitated, but I knew what she was going to ask. If I'd made my decision.

"I cannot leave the light unattended," I said. "And I won't leave Papa. He seems strong, but he isn't. He needs me."

I watched for Papa as long as there was daylight, and then climbed the tower steps to light the lamps. I'd seen Papa do it a thousand times, no, three thousand times, and I'd even helped him do it, but still, my hands shook as I held the match to the wicks.

Margaret put Celia to bed. I heard her singing:

> *On wings of the wind o'er the dark rolling deep,*
> *angels are coming to watch o'er thy sleep.*
> *Angels are coming to watch over thee,*
> *so list to the wind coming over the sea.*
> *Hear the wind blow, love, hear the wind blow.*
> *Lean your head over and hear the wind blow.*

I wandered back down to the kitchen. Margaret joined me and we sat, not speaking, listening to the tick-tick-tick of the clock, and the wind, but I was listening more for the creak of Papa's oarlocks, and the sound of the skiff scraping against the rocks. Sleep tugged at my eyelids. My head nodded, once, twice, and then Papa was in the room, smelling of salt and the sea, and even though I was fourteen and almost as tall as he, I ran into his arms and buried my face against his chest.

"The light guided me home," he said. "I knew I could count on you, Quila."

"We were worried about you, Franklin," Margaret said. I couldn't remember her using his first name before.

"No need," Papa said. "I brought you something." He stepped outside and came back carrying a pail. Papa tipped the pail onto Margaret's lap, and blueberries tumbled out, filling her apron.

"I wish they were emeralds," he said. Margaret looked dazed.

"You went to pick blueberries?" she said.

"That," Papa said, "and to work up the nerve to ask you to be my wife."

It took a moment for his words to sink in, for both Margaret and me.

"It's as hard as that, is it?" Margaret said.

"Thinking of a life with me?" Papa shook his head.

"What's hard is the life you'd be agreeing to. I'm more married to this light than to any woman, with nothing to offer but long hours and loneliness, little pay and even less place to spend it."

"Sure, and you've given me plenty of reasons to say no," Margaret said. "Can you give me one reason to say yes?"

Papa was quiet so long I didn't think he was going to answer her. Then he took her hand, and she rose to follow him. I trailed along behind. Papa led Margaret out to the cliffs, where the moonlight spilled onto the sea.

"That Land of Light where the fairies live," Papa said. "What did it take to keep the door open?"

"Metal," Margaret said. "A piece of metal formed by human hands."

"Like this?" Papa said, and moonlight glinted off the ring he held in his hand. Above him, the tower flashed its light far out into the darkness.

"The Land of Light," he said. "I'm hoping you've found it right here."

CHAPTER 12

Papa and Margaret were married a week later, on a day when the weather was fine enough for us to row over to the mainland to find a minister.

Before the ceremony, Margaret gave Celia a small mother-of-pearl comb.

"This was your mother's, when she was little," she said. "Someday I'll tell you all about her."

To me, she gave a jar of sea glass, bits of red and blue and green.

"When I first came to Devils Rock, I could tell you liked sea glass by the pieces I found on the windowsill

in your room. I've been collecting them for you ever since."

I held it up to the light, and the colors sparkled like jewels, one shade of blue like Mama's eyes, another like Margaret's.

Mr. and Mrs. Richardson came to the wedding. Mrs. Richardson clasped Margaret's hand.

"You make sure that husband of yours brings you by to visit now and then," Mrs. Richardson said. "It can get pretty lonely out there."

I felt Margaret's other hand tighten around my waist.

"Oh, I shan't be lonely, Mrs. Richardson," she said "I've got my family now."

After the wedding, Papa hired a horse and buggy and we drove into the highlands of Maine. Everything was new to Celia and me, and we squealed at each new sight—mountains and rivers, deer and rabbit and moose—and I felt my heart pound to see the trees, especially the maples. They were every shade of orange and yellow and red, even more beautiful than Mama had promised. Papa pointed out spruce and fir and hemlock, and we ate our picnic lunch under trees with white bark that curled and peeled. Papa said they were birches.

While Celia napped, I slipped away into the woods and lay under a golden canopy of leaves.

In my whole life, I'd never been where I couldn't hear the sea; it was like a second heartbeat to me. Here, under the trees, there was no wind, no pounding surf, only the soft chitter of songbirds.

Using my hands and a stick, I dug up two small spruce trees and brought them back to the picnic spot.

"What are those for?" Margaret asked.

"One for Mama's grave," I said. "And one for your sister." As soon as I'd said it, I was sorry because Margaret began to cry.

"They're tears of happiness, silly," Margaret said, hugging me. "Oh, how did I ever get so lucky to find the three of you?" But I think we're the lucky ones.

The sea brought us Celia and it brought us Margaret. We're a family, and there's no greater treasure than that.

This book was inspired by a true story that happened off Hendricks Head Lighthouse near Boothbay Harbor, Maine. In the mid-1800s, following a terrible storm, a lighthouse keeper did see a bundle floating in the water and found a baby girl inside. The keeper and his wife adopted the girl and raised her as their own.

I was sitting at my desk one day, working on another book, when the first sentence of this book came into my head. I wrote it down, set it aside, and continued to work on the other story. But a girl's voice came to me, Aquila's voice, and said, "Tell my story. Now."

I have tried to do just that.

NATALIE KINSEY-WARNOCK is the author of several books for young readers, including *The Canada Geese Quilt*, which was an ALA Notable Book, a *Booklist* Editors' Choice, and an NCSS-CBC Notable Children's Trade Book in the Field of Social Studies. Her deep love of the natural world is evident in all of her writing and was formed early on while growing up in Vermont, where she still lives with her husband and their many dogs, cats, and horses. To learn more about Natalie, visit her Web site at www.kinsey-warnock.com.